Santa's Autograph

To:

From Santa:

✗
_____

Date:

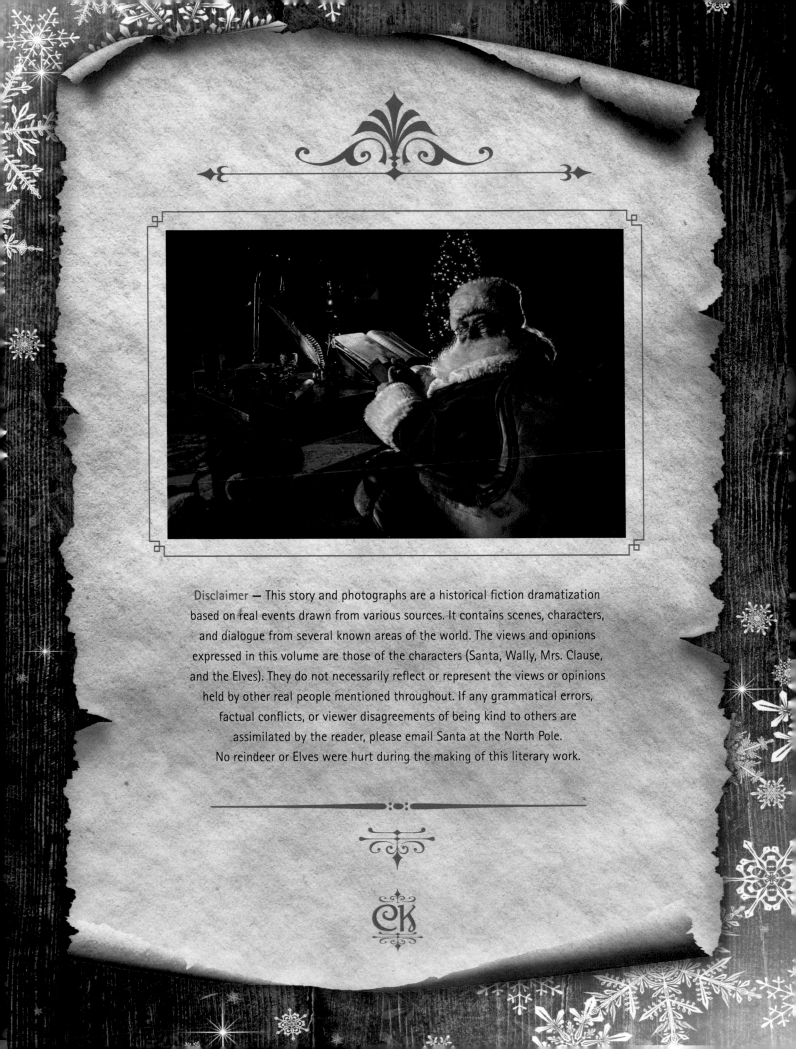

Dear Friends,

I'm sorry this book has taken me so many years
to write. I've been busy the past hundred years
of my life, but I finally found the time to explain
my journey. Thank you for patiently waiting,
and I hope you enjoy learning about me.
My wish is that you will have fun while reading
this and make the world a better place.
Adults and children will now find out some of
my secrets to understand how I became Santa.
Have a Merry Christmas and a Happy New Year!

— Chris Kringle

I was born on January 1, 1900, more than a hundred years ago. My picture was seen on the front page of The New York Times newspaper because nurses delivered me seconds after midnight on New Year's Day.
The name given to me when I arrived was Christopher Clause Kringle.

When I was little, my mother read books to me every night. She taught me how to listen and also how to pay attention. The doctors thought I was the smartest child in New York City because my parents taught me how to read and write at a very young age.

The New York Times

The New York Times   NEW YORK, MONDAY, JANUARY 1, 1900

Chris Kringle, the son of Luke and Natasha Kringle, was born Monday, January 1, 1900.

THE CENTURY'S FIRST BABY IS BORN!

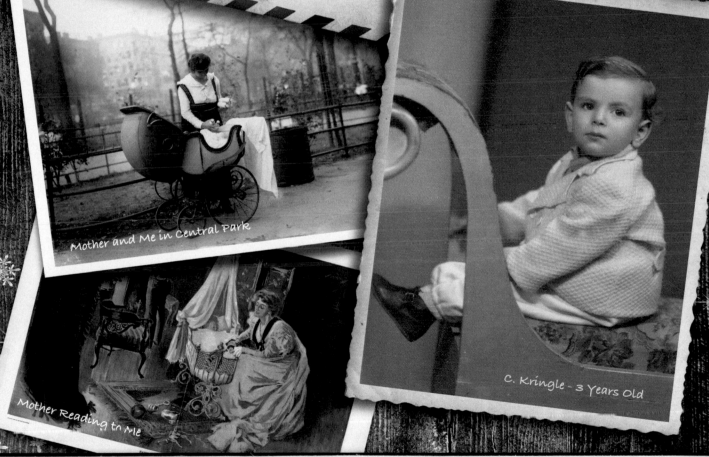

Mother and Me in Central Park

Mother Reading to Me

C. Kringle - 3 Years Old

New York City - 1900

When I was a little boy, kids didn't have all of the toys and games that we have today. We didn't have video games, stuffed animals, Barbies, iPhones, or even computers. My friends and I played with marbles and jacks. We skipped around town and played hopscotch and leapfrog. We even danced around the maypole and sang "Ring-around-the-Rosie."

As a child, I wished that we had more exciting games to play. In the early 1900s, we didn't have many fun options.

Hop Scotch

Maypole

Leap Frog

Marbles

Ring-around-the-Rosie

Kids Having Fun

When I was five, my father took me to work with him in Pennsylvania to the Hershey chocolate factory. One of the buildings had an electrical fire, but my dad and I put it out with baking soda (not baking powder). After I helped save the factory, Mr. Hershey offered me a job for five-cents an hour, which was a lot of money back then. I also got to eat all the chocolate I wanted for free.

My father and Mr. Hershey taught me that children should be educated. They said that most kids my age worked all day long and didn't go to school. Mr. Hershey was like a second father to me and taught me lots of things.

My Cousin Eating Chocolate

Building on Fire

Mr. Milton S. Hershey

HERSHEY'S
REG. U. S. PAT. OFF.
Tropical
CHOCOLATE

That summer in 1905, my mother took me
to see my Aunt Shirley in New Jersey. She lived
on a "Magic Farm" where I learned how to feed
the animals, sew clothing, cook food, wash
clothes, hang laundry, and milk the cows.
My Aunt Shirley said I was the best worker
she had ever seen. It was on her farm where
I met my best friend in the world—Wally.

As an adult, I still like to milk the cows.
This is something that my wife and I
would later teach the Elves.

THE OLD FARM HOUSE

Wife and Me Milking Cows, 1980

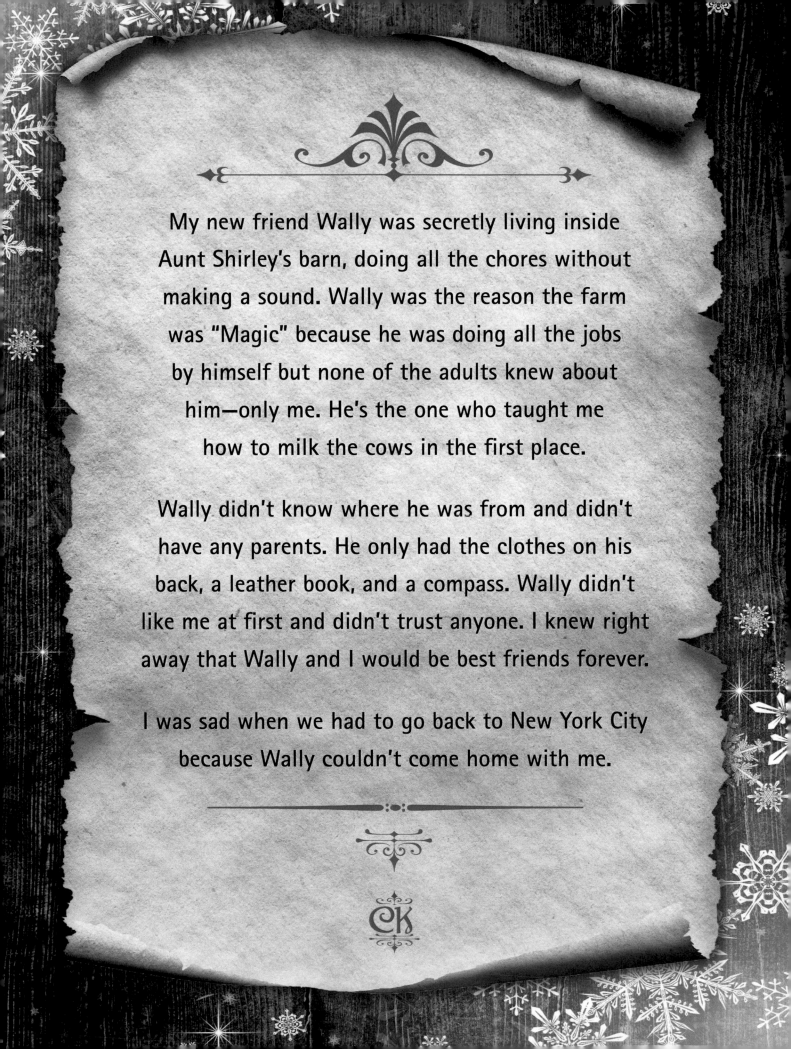

My new friend Wally was secretly living inside
Aunt Shirley's barn, doing all the chores without
making a sound. Wally was the reason the farm
was "Magic" because he was doing all the jobs
by himself but none of the adults knew about
him—only me. He's the one who taught me
how to milk the cows in the first place.

Wally didn't know where he was from and didn't
have any parents. He only had the clothes on his
back, a leather book, and a compass. Wally didn't
like me at first and didn't trust anyone. I knew right
away that Wally and I would be best friends forever.

I was sad when we had to go back to New York City
because Wally couldn't come home with me.

Wally

Wally's Compass and Journal

Wally's Home

Thanks to Mr. Hershey, in 1905 my mother took me on a train to Washington D.C. to meet the President of the United States. His name was Theodore Roosevelt, but he asked me to call him Teddy. We had one very important topic to discuss—*education*. At that time, children worked all day long and didn't go to school. Most kids my age didn't know how to read or write—but I did. I shared my concerns with President Teddy about kids not going to school. We agreed that children are the future and everyone deserves the opportunity to learn. This is why we started the Public Education school system.

President Theodore Roosevelt

White House - 1905

Textile Workers

Cotton Mill

By the time I was six, my parents had found out about Wally living in Aunt Shirley's barn. They adopted my best friend, and we moved into a bigger house in Queens. Now I had my best friend living with me. Wally got to go to school instead of working on a farm. I got to go to school instead of working in a factory or selling newspapers. We both knew how lucky we were to be learning inside a classroom. I taught Wally how to read and write, and he taught me how to have fun. We played all sorts of new games like hide-n-go-seek, kick-the-can, and my favorite game: ding-dong-ditch. I've always liked hiding games where people can't find me.

Even though we argue sometimes, I love my brother and my family more than anything. Wally and I are happy we are both brothers and best friends.

Recess

New York - East Side Eviction (1.2) 304-6

Moving Day

Wally and Me

OFFEE CAKE

LUNCH ROOM

The Morning Telegraph

Waking Up Early to Sell Newspapers

My Classroom

Growing up in New York City, Wally and I saw that other people have different colored hair, many shades of skin, and different colored eyes. My parents taught Wally and me that everyone on planet Earth is unique, but each of us is exactly the same—on the inside. We all have different features that make each of us beautiful in our own special way.

"It's good to be different," my mother would always say. "Everyone has a skill of their own," my father would tell Wally and me.

Our parents also taught us lots of different languages so we could talk to and be friends with other kids that lived nearby.

Children Are the Future

When I was seven, children didn't receive any
presents under the Christmas tree. Most families
were poor and didn't have much money. Christmas
was celebrated as the birth of Jesus Christ—a holy
day. Most people would go to church and eat dinner
with family, but there were no gifts exchanged.
I wanted to add presents to this holiday celebration
so Christmas could be more fun and exciting for kids.

The next year in 1908, I saved my earnings from
the Hershey factory and bought some gifts for
my parents and Wally. I thought it would be
a nice gesture to hide wrapped boxes under
our tree without anyone knowing.

XMAS TOYS

942-3

Window Shopping

No Presents Under the Tree

LOAD OF XMAS TREES, N.Y.

That Christmas Eve, I secretly put gifts under our tree for the very first time. I even gave a box to myself, so no one knew the presents were from me. I was taught at an early age that it's better to give than to receive, which is why I gave the gifts to my family in the first place. I really enjoyed surprising my parents and Wally with the perfect items they desired.

Over the next couple of years, I decided to surprise all the children that lived nearby. Everyone wondered who was giving presents to all the girls and boys. Some people weren't happy with my new Christmas idea because a few adults thought a burglar was breaking into their home. But I kept giving gifts anyway because I knew how excited it made everyone, especially the children.

1st Rocking Horse I Ever Made

Presents Under the Tree

More Presents Under the Tree

Sledding in Central Park

Later that year, our father showed Wally and me how to build things in the garage. We also started repairing items for friends and neighbors after school. We sewed clothing, fixed bicycles, and even repaired shoes. I also made two bikes—one for Wally and one for me. The other thing we liked to fix was a new invention called the "radio" which first played music on Christmas Eve in 1906. We loved listening to songs in our garage. The radio was a magical listening device because we could hear music, news, and sports from far away places.

In our garage, Wally and I also learned how to make costumes so we could play hide-and-seek better with our friends.

Dad Falling Off Bike

Fixing a Bike

Our Garage and Radio

Shoe Repair

Fixing Radios

I learned how to create things from working with my father. In 1908, I helped Henry Ford with his assembly line. Mr. Ford was so grateful for my assistance that he gave me one of the first Model T automobiles. It's a good thing we had the car because Wally and I liked to drink Coca-Cola and we had to drive all over town to find it. When we were kids, this drink was not available like it is today. Only a few places in New York sold it because it was mostly seen in Atlanta, Georgia, where it was made.

During December, I started driving all around New York City to deliver presents to family and friends. I chose Christmas Eve to deliver gifts because I knew adults and children would be sleeping. While all the kids were happy, there was one problem that was starting to occur. Certain newspapers were trying to find out who the person was delivering presents on Christmas Eve.

Ford Assembly Line

Ford Model-T

My First Car

One weekend when I was eleven, I went to work with my father in Baltimore. I got into an accident while driving my car too fast and crashed. While the car was getting fixed, my father had me go to a stricter school for boys.

During this time in the early 1900s, there was no age limit for children to drive. There was no driving test, no license plates, and the whole state of New York didn't have stop signs or a single traffic light.

After the car was repaired, Wally and I painted it red—because that's my favorite color. My favorite number is 57, in case you wanted to know. Wally's favorite number is 42, and he likes the color blue.

Crashed My Car - Baltimore

Fixed Car and Painted it Red

At St. Mary's School in Baltimore, while my car was getting fixed, I met a boy named George who liked to play baseball. George wasn't very good, but I taught him how to hit and pitch. We practiced every day after school until he got better. George later became famous and played for the Boston Red Sox and the New York Yankees. He is better known as George Herman "Babe" Ruth and is one of the best players in baseball history. He hit more home runs than anyone and visited sick children in the hospital all the time.

George as a Pitcher

Ruth with Children

Traded to Yankees

Ruth Bows Out. Yankees Retiring #3 - 1948

Red Sox Slugger

Home Run King

During my teenage years, I continued to deliver presents to family and friends while no one knew it was me, not even Wally. I never got caught sneaking into homes, sliding down chimneys, or climbing through windows; I always had creative ways to get in.

Kids in my neighborhood would receive presents—if they were good. Children liked to hang up their stockings by the fireplace to let me know they had behaved well that year.

The newspaper reporters were still trying to find out who was breaking and entering. They asked the police to look out for a robber they called "The Christmas Eve Burglar." Parents and children were happy because nothing was ever stolen, only presents, games, and toys were left in people's homes—under their trees.

CK

N.Y. Police Hdqrs - Information Bure
Police discussing "Christmas Eve Burglar"

339-7

Christmas Eve

Police and Search Dogs

Firemen Question Me - 1930

Looking for Santa

During my twenties, I met the girl of my dreams. Her name was Norene. She was a flapper, or a performer, who loved to dance and sing. After Wally caught me delivering toys, I finally told my family that I was the one giving gifts at Christmastime. They agreed to keep my secret and help me with my gift giving mission.

Wally asked my girlfriend Norene to help us deliver presents that year. My mom and Norene began making lists to stay organized. In the garage, Wally, my father, and I built all the toys. It was a family business at first, but we needed to know what children wanted as presents. That's when my mother and Norene asked kids to start writing us letters. When children behaved and did well in school, we liked to give presents on Christmas morning.

Mrs. Clause - 1924

LETTERS

Letter for Santa Clause

LETTERS FOR SANTA

Writing to Santa Clause, 12/4/20

It was during the Roaring Twenties that we made lots
of money with one special gift for President Roosevelt.
To this day, our present still remains a secret because it's
a famous toy that we made when President Teddy passed
away. People around the world wanted to purchase this
new gift that my family had created. Everyone enjoyed
this item, which led to sales in the millions. Then we
bought some land, started a factory, and hired lots
of people. We needed to mass produce this special
gift so everyone in the world could have one.

All of a sudden our Kringle family was wealthy.
We were able to afford several more cars and trucks
for our business. We had so many toys to make
and deliver, I even got my pilot license and learned
to fly airplanes. Now, Wally and I could fly all
around the world. This was when we discovered
the Elves and the North Pole.

Teddy Bears

Getting Pilot's License - 1927

Flying School and Present Delivery

5027

We were very excited when we got to meet the leader Elf named Jingle. The 1029 Elves in the village didn't call me Chris Kringle. They gave me the Elf name Santa, which means "holy" and combined it with my middle name Clause. It was in the Village of Elf where I was first called Santa Clause.

Since the beginning of time, the Elves have lived at the North Pole. They believed they were the only people on planet Earth. No one could ever find the Elves because they lived in tunnels—rooted deep under the snow.

The Elves are very good at building tunnels, but they didn't know how to read or write. They worked hard all day long, and didn't find time to have any fun. Wally and I taught the Elves many games. They especially love playing hide-and-seek with us.

Village of Elf

Tunnels Under Village

Northern Lights

NORTH POLE

Although the Elves and the reindeer both lived at the North Pole, they were scared of each other. When Wally and I tried to introduce them, the Elves ran away and hid while the reindeer jumped high in the sky.

I would later find out that some of these reindeer had hollow bones—just like birds, which is how they can fly. The reindeer's powerful legs are so strong that they can jump up and take off like a rocket.

Seeing the reindeer leap, I had an idea. Wally thought I was crazy, but I decided to get on the reindeer's back like a horse. Instead of galloping, the reindeer took off in the air and we went flying. It was so much fun. When we landed, Jingle and the Elves were lined up waiting for a turn—they loved it too!

The reindeer enjoyed taking the Elves on rides and both were excited to be flying. The Elves weren't afraid of the reindeer anymore and wanted to do something nice for their new friends.

Reindeer Training

Reindeer Training

Gathering Reindeer

1st Flight

As a gift for the rides, the Elves began to help the reindeer find food. The Elves used their shovels and tools to dig through the deep snow. By doing this, the Reindeer could eat more seeds, berries, and worms—all things birds like to eat. I was starting to think this unique species of deer were just large birds.

Once the Elves and reindeer became friends they started to develop a symbiotic relationship. The Elves helped the reindeer dig to get to their food more easily. While the reindeer helped the Elves travel above ground and carry heavy loads of supplies to the village.

This was also when the Elves started to help us make toys for the children around the world, even though lots of kids still wondered who I was.

Feeding Reindeer

Little Betty Sze,
Daughter of the
Minister from China

Some Kids Didn't Recognize Me

Santa was the reason the Elves and the reindeer became friends.

One night, Wally and I saw several reindeer jump as a group. They liked to fly from one mountain top to another mountain top in the cold icy snow. After each takeoff, they always came down and needed to land—which they did quietly and precisely every time. Watching the reindeer jump around together, I had the idea for them to help us deliver toys instead of using cars, trucks, and planes.

Most people don't know that before the reindeer got involved, I used dogsleds and turkeys to help pull my sleigh in areas of the world where there weren't any roads.

Reindeer Jumping from
Mountain Top to Mountain Top

Turkeys Pulling Sled

Dogs Pulling Sled

A Load of Xmas Packages

In 1947, I built a weightless magnetic sleigh for the reindeer to help us with our gift-giving mission. We loaded the sleigh with presents, but it wasn't heavy at all—even though it was filled with toys.

The reindeer loved helping me pull the sleigh because they are rewarded with lots of food, which is scarce at the North Pole. Then we discovered the reindeer like carrots and apples too. One secret that no one knows is that reindeer like to eat grapes in the middle of winter, when they are hardest to find.

When the Christmas season is over our work is still not done. Wally and I need to repair the sleigh every year, always making it better, faster, and safer.

Magnetic Weightless Sleigh

Looking for Rudolph

Flying Through Trees

Delivering presents with the reindeer was quick, magical, and exciting. We now had millions of presents to deliver. We were starting to receive letters from people all over the world. Everyone in different countries was now writing to us: children, teenagers, adults—even the President's wife. First Lady Eleanor Roosevelt wanted to meet me because she liked helping children too.

This was an incredible time because the special reindeer and the magnetic sleigh could land on rooftops without making a sound. We started becoming even more famous in the 1940s because movies and television began sharing our story.

Pile of Letters to Santa

Kids Watching Television

Meeting Eleanor Roosevelt

Joan Wilson Confides in Santa

Visiting Santa for the 1st Time

In 1955, we came up with an even better idea for our deliveries. Wally and I divided up the globe into eight regions we called "Drop Zones." We discussed hiding presents in separate secret locations, in all different nations around the world. Our goal was to give a gift to each and every child in just one evening.

Wally said we needed to find a way to get the job done quickly, and I wanted to continue being sneaky. This new system would help us accomplish both goals. We estimated that it would take five hours per drop zone, but now we had to find good hiding spots for all the toys.

DROP ZONES

Boy with Polio Coming to Meet Me

Looking for Santa Clause

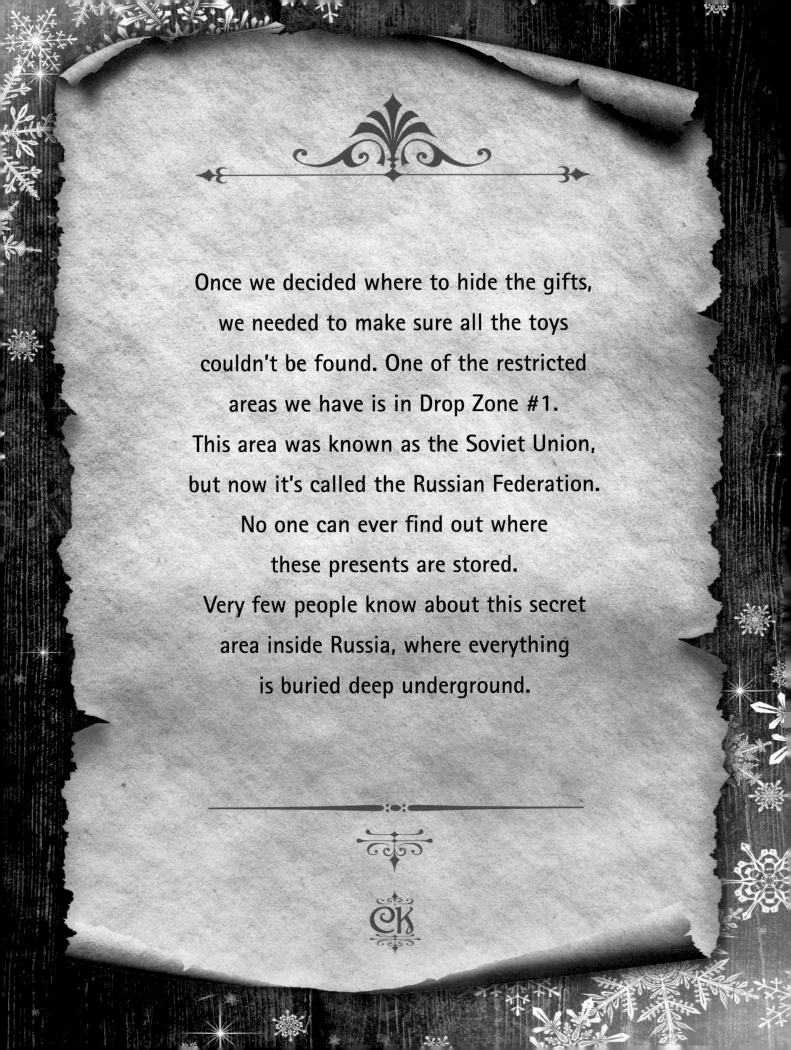

Once we decided where to hide the gifts,
we needed to make sure all the toys
couldn't be found. One of the restricted
areas we have is in Drop Zone #1.
This area was known as the Soviet Union,
but now it's called the Russian Federation.
No one can ever find out where
these presents are stored.
Very few people know about this secret
area inside Russia, where everything
is buried deep underground.

Rainbow in Russia

Winter in Moscow

Secret Area in Russia

The location of Drop Zone #2 is high up in the mountains near the Great Wall of China. We have lots of presents to deliver all over India and Asia.

In Drop Zone #3, we use an old military base known as Fort Drum. It's in the Philippines, which has over 7500 islands. It only takes a few seconds to jump to Australia and deliver presents to all the children there.

In Drop Zone #4, our secret hiding spot is in the Congo. Here in Africa, sometimes the animals get in our way—especially on the island of Madagascar. We like to bring the animals presents too, in the form of food. We found that zebras and giraffes love to eat carrots and apples—just like the reindeer.

Africa

China

Christmas in Africa

Baby Elephants

Zebra and Giraffes

In Drop Zone #5, our hiding spot for Europe is in France under the Eiffel Tower. It's the perfect place for the reindeer to land and take off because the Elves help Wally move presents up and down this tall structure.

It only takes the reindeer two jumps to fly to Norway, Sweden, and Finland. Deliveries here are completed in under four hours! I like the slanted rooftops in Germany because of the easy access to all the chimneys.

France

Italy

England

Spain

Germany

Drop Zone #6 is in Peru. There is a hidden spot in South America near Machu Picchu.

Drop Zones #7 and #8 are related, but no one can know precisely where. I'll give you a hint if you keep it a secret—one is in Los Angeles, California, and the other is in Orlando, Florida. Wally and I have to keep this area private for matters of national security. All the presents are kept underground in a place you already know. These two drop zones hold enough toys for all the children in Canada, the United States, Mexico, and Central America combined!

Having hidden areas to store toys is how we restock the sleigh without having to go back to the North Pole. This allows us to cover a large area in a short amount of time. The company FedEx uses a similar delivery system when packages have to be delivered all over world— also overnight.

Peru

Mexico

Seaplane in Central America

FEDERAL EXPRESS

In 1957, Norene and I got married and moved to the North Pole so we could live a really long time. Wally and his wife come to visit us every two weeks, but they come by seaplane, then use the train.

We all love the chilly cold climate. It is one of the reasons why we will live until the year 2200. How we live longer is similar to putting food in the refrigerator to keep things fresh. The same applies to us humans, and that's why we live here, so we can hopefully live forever. I think we can live at least three-hundred years, but Wally has his doubts.

Adults have always asked me—how can people remain alive for this long? There are many secrets that we've learned from the Elves. One is to eat healthy, get regular exercise, and don't let stress bother you.

1950s Refrigerator

Wally Coming to Visit

North Pole Express

North Pole Express

Wally Teasing Me

After Mrs. Clause and I were settled in our new home, we had another massive job to do. None of the Elves had any real homes or knew how to cook their food. All the Elves ate was raw fish and boiled snow for water. That's all they had in their cold Arctic world. Everything that I had learned in the past, we needed to teach the Elves. We taught them how to build homes, how to grow fruits and vegetables in greenhouses, and we even started a school for young Elflings.

Then we built the ultimate production facility in the world. The Elves called this new warehouse—Santa's Workshop. It is a magical place where the Elves can make anything they can imagine—like Wally and I did in our old garage.

At first, the Elves liked to build bikes, because that's what I first made as a child. But now, the Elves like to build new toys for the children of today.

Sewing

Factory

Factory

SOMEWHERE AROUND THE
NORTH
POLE
MAP

ARCTIC OCEAN

Sleigh Garage

Gingerbread House

Christmas Music Academy

Post Office

Polar Bear Orphanage

Toy Factory

Elf Village

North Pole Café

Santa's Home

Reindeer Stables

Over the years, these are the best gifts that we've given each decade. It seems like long ago, but these are my favorite presents since I've been alive.

1900s – Bikes (the first thing I built)
1910s – Ice Skates, Rocking Horse, Yo-Yo
1920s – Sleds, Wagons, Teddy Bears
1930s – Raggedy Ann Doll, Toy-Trains, Army Men
1940s – Matchbox Cars, Doll Houses, Slinky
1950s – Baseball Cards, Barbies, Mr. Potato Head
1960s – G.I. Joes, Etch-A-Sketch, Easy-Bake Oven
1970s – Atari, Rubik's Cube, Star Wars Action Figures
1980s – Nintendo, Transformers, Cabbage Patch Dolls
1990s – Beanie Babies, Tickle Me Elmo, Furby
2000s – Playstation/Xbox/Nintendo Wii
2010s – iPhone, iPad
2020s – Playstation 5 and more to come...

Playstation 5

Presents

My New Phone

Girl with Drone

There are many secrets about the Elves and the reindeer that most people do not know. First of all, Elves can live forever, but they only grow four feet tall. They are sneaky little people who are very hard to find. They are so quick and speedy, that it's impossible to take their picture.

The North Pole reindeer are just large birds. They sleep in nests, fly south for the winter, and their poop is white—*just like birds*. When reindeer eat seeds, berries, and leaves, their poop has little red spots—which looks disgusting! But the Elves like to eat reindeer poop and consider it a delicacy. The Elves told me that it tastes wonderful, so I tried a bite, and it tastes exactly like peppermint bark.

The Elves' favorite food is reindeer poop, which is very hard to find—especially around Christmastime. The Elves also love candy, but it's not good for their teeth. For all their hard work, once a week during December, Mrs. Clause invites the Elves into her "Sweet Shoppe" in the Village of Elf to eat as much candy as they want.

Reindeer Poop, Candy Cane, and Hot Chocolate

When we were younger, Wally and I were never good at sports. But we liked to help those children who would be great at something. We always want to give presents that can help a good girl or boy succeed in life.

During the depression, in 1931, one young curly-haired girl wanted a Raggedy Anne doll for Christmas. But I got her singing, acting, and dancing lessons instead. This little girl became famous, starred in movies, and now there is a kid's drink named after her.

In 1939, one little boy named Mickey from Oklahoma wanted a basketball for Christmas. I gave him a baseball bat, not by error. When Mickey got older, he won seven World Series titles and three-MVPs in his magnificent switch-hitting career.

In 1955, a British lad named Paul wanted a trumpet when he was a teen. He got a left-handed guitar, started a band with his friends, and later bought a yellow submarine.

In 1966, another little boy named Joe from Pennsylvania wanted a basketball and hoop. I gave him a football for Christmas, and he learned to throw it with his dad. Joe won four Super Bowls for a team in my favorite color and became the best quarterback ever.

In 1987, two sisters growing up in Los Angeles wanted dolls and clothing for Christmas one year. They got new tennis racquets and became the best players the court has ever seen.

In 1993, I thought a little boy from Argentina wanted a Lionel Train because of his name. When I saw him he got a soccer ball instead. Now everyone just calls him the GOAT, which means the Greatest of all Time.

Shirley Temple

Paul McCartney

The Beatles

Mickey Mantle

Joe Montana

Lionel Messi

Williams Sisters

With some of my Santa secrets now revealed, the favorite gift that I've ever received is when Rudolph was born in 1939. The other two most important events in my life—are the day I met Wally and the day I married my wife.

Have you been good this year? Do you know what you want for Christmas? Please write to me, or email the Elves who are now learning to type.

We always want to acknowledge children who have been nice to others, so we can help you do great things in life.

Rudolph

Christmas Magic

My family and Wally's family celebrate Christmas together. I understand that not everyone observes this holiday, and that's okay. I just want everyone to know that giving gifts is our way of spreading the message about peace and being kind.

I want all the children of the world to understand:
It doesn't matter where you live.
It doesn't matter what religion you believe in.
It doesn't matter what you look like,
or any other differences we have.
The only thing that matters is how
we treat others and ourselves.
I just want us all to love each other and be kind.

Naughty or Nice List

Wishing You Well

Our mission is world peace.

We hope you will join us with our goal.

The End

This story is based on the Christopher Kringle book series coming out soon. Please see www.chriskringle.com for more details and release dates.

Santa's Life Story
Young Adult Book Series

Christopher Kringle & The Darkness of Light (1897–1906)
Christopher Kringle & The Journal of Life (1905–1909)
Christopher Kringle & The Hidden Treasure (1910–1915)
Christopher Kringle & The Murderer's Row (1916–1929)
Christopher Kringle & The Keys to Life (1930–1934)
Christopher Kringle & The Evils of War (1935–1941)
Christopher Kringle & The Great Escapes (1942–1946)
Christopher Kringle & The Angels of Death (1947–1957)
*** (written not titled) (1957–1967)
*** (written not titled) (1967–1987)

HINT—This book series is for adults too. Historical fiction with a twist of Christmas without the religion. It's good versus evil, using real people while educating at the same time. Chris and Wally will find a way to solve humanity's biggest problems, while the bad guys continue to claim they don't exist. Many secrets from around the world will now be revealed.

Santa loves photos, which is why there will
always be pictures in his books!

Santa now has a cell phone.
You cannot call him, but you can ask him questions.

Email Your Letter To Santa:

cckringle1900@gmail.com

Or visit:

www.chriskringle.com

Photo Credits - In Order

Kids having fun: Two Boys Playing, [Between 1909 and 1923] Photograph. https://www.loc.gov/item/2016820419
Leap frog: Leap-Frog. Photograph. Library of Congress, <www.loc.gov/item/2006675916
Hop-scotch: Hop-Scotch, Photograph. Library of Congress, <www.loc.gov/item/2004677389
Marbles: Marble Time. Photograph. Library of Congress, <www.loc.gov/item/2006675917
Mulberry Bush: Here we go 'round the Mulberry Bush, Photograph. <www.loc.gov/item/2004677388
Maypole: Detroit Publishing Co., Publisher. May pole dance, Central Park, NY, Photograph. https://www.loc.gov/item/2016811301
Mr. Milton S. Hershey: Wikimedia Commons, This media file is in the public domain.
Hershey Tropical Chocolate Bar: Wikimedia Commons, This media file is in the public domain.
Building on fire: Harris & Ewing, photographer. Building Fire. 1928. Photograph. https://www.loc.gov/item/2016888851
Farm house; Kelly, Thomas, The Old Farm House, 1874, Photograph. https://www.loc.gov/item/2003662884
Milking cows – 1980: Highsmith, Carol M, United States, Photograph. https://www.loc.gov/item/2011634988
Teddy: President Theodore Roosevelt nearly full face, 1902. Photograph. https://www.loc.gov/item/97504551
White House – 1905: Harris & Ewing, photographer. White House, Library of Congress, www.loc.gov/item/2016855752
Textile Workers: Library of Congress, Prints & Photographs Division, National Child Labor Committee Collection, [LC-DIG-nclc-02557]
Cotton Mill: Library of Congress, Prints & Photographs Division, National Child Labor Committee Collection, [LC-DIG-nclc-01537]
Recess: Harris & Ewing, photographer. HOLTON ARMS SCHOOL PLAYGROUND, Photograph. https://www.loc.gov/item/2016861828
Moving Day: Bain News Service, Publisher. New York, East Side eviction, Photograph. https://www.loc.gov/item/2014681356
Newspapers: Photo by Lewis W. Hine. NY, NY, 1908. February. Photograph. https://www.loc.gov/item/2018673665
My classroom: Johnston, Frances Benjamin, photographer. Washington, D.C. 1899, https://www.loc.gov/item/2001703721
Window shopping: Bain News Service, Publisher. Photograph. https://www.loc.gov/item/2014684429
No presents under the tree: Christmas Tree, [Between 1910 and 1935] Photograph. https://www.loc.gov/item/2016824592
Load of xmas trees – N.Y.: Bain News Service, Publisher. 1910, Photograph. https://www.loc.gov/item/2014689328
Presents under the tree: Wilbur & Orville Wright, photographer. Dayton Ohio, 1900. Photograph. https://www.loc.gov/item/2001696299
More presents under the tree: Hauck Christmas tree. [Between 1910 and 1935] Photograph. https://www.loc.gov/item/2016824899
Central Park: Detroit Publishing Co., Publisher, Byron, photographer, NY, NY 1900. Photograph. https://www.loc.gov/item/2016808726
Fixing radio: Underwood & Underwood, Library of Congress's Prints and Photographs division under the digital ID cph.3b25191
Dad falling off bike: What happened? Frost, A. B., Artist. 1897, Photograph, https://www.loc.gov/item/2010715933
Ford: Assembly line at the Ford Motor Company's Highland Park plant, 1913. Photograph. https://www.loc.gov/item/2011661021
Ford Model-T: Early Ford automobile, 1908. Photograph. https://www.loc.gov/item/2011660900
Crashed my car: Auto Accident, 1922, Photograph. https://www.loc.gov/item/2016832851
Ruth with children: Bain News Service, Publisher. Babe Ruth, New York AL baseball, 1921. Photograph. https://www.loc.gov/item/2014712537
George as a pitcher: Francis P. Burke Collection, 1914 and 1919. This work is in the public domain.
Red Sox slugger: Babe Ruth, Gift; Herbert A. French, 1919. Photograph. https://www.loc.gov/item/2016827094
Traded to Yankees: wikimedia commons, This media file is in the public domain in the United States.
Home Run King: Irwin, La Broad, & Pudlin, wikimedia commons, This work is in the public domain because it was published before Jan. 1, 1925.
Ruth Bows out: Nathaniel Fein, Originally published in the New York Herald Tribune, 1948, This work is in the public domain.
Police discussing: New York City Police Dept. 1908. Photograph. https://www.loc.gov/item/2006677372
Christmas Eve: Christmas Eve. Photograph. Retrieved from the Library of Congress, <www.loc.gov/item/95506187
Police and search dogs: Bain News Service, Publisher. 1912, Photograph. https://www.loc.gov/item/2014680003
Firemen question me: Santa Claus story, 12/6/21, 1921. Photograph. https://www.loc.gov/item/2016831818
Looking for Santa: Where Santa Claus lives, 1900. Photograph. https://www.loc.gov/item/89714979
Letter for Santa Claus: Bain News Service, Publisher. 1910. Photograph. https://www.loc.gov/item/2014689327
Writing to Santa Claus, 12/4/20: Gift; Herbert A. French; 12/4/20. , 1920, Photograph. https://www.loc.gov/item/2016829325
Getting pilot's license: Harris & Ewing, photographer, 1927 November or December],LC-DIG-hec-34635
Flying school: Santa Claus in aeroplane, 1921. Herbert A. French Photograph. https://www.loc.gov/item/2016845227
Reindeer training 1: Lomen Bros, photographer. Alaska, https://www.loc.gov/item/99614708/. Gift; Mrs. W. Chapin Huntington; 1951
Reindeer training 2: Gift; Mrs. W. Chapin Huntington; 1951. Alaska US, 1900, Photograph. https://www.loc.gov/item/99615160
Gathering Reindeer: Traveling by reindeer, Archangel, Russia, 1890, Photograph. https://www.loc.gov/item/2001697540
Little Betty Sze: daughter of the minister from China and Madam Sze; 1921. Photograph. https://www.loc.gov/item/92517492
Some kids didn't recognize me: https://www.floridamemory.com/items/show/81588, image is in the public domain.
Turkeys: Photo originally copyrighted by Schrader & Dennis, Three Oaks, Mich, 1909. Photograph. https://www.loc.gov/item/2005686533
Truckload of presents: Bain News Service, Publisher, 1913. Photograph. https://www.loc.gov/item/2014689398
Magnetic weightless sleigh: Bain News Service, publisher, 1880-1890, Photograph. https://www.loc.gov/item/2015651615
Pile of letters to Santa: https://www.floridamemory.com/items/show/68291, image is in the public domain.
Eleanor Roosevelt: Harris & Ewing, photographer. Washington D.C, 1938. Photograph. https://www.loc.gov/item/2016883843
Kids watching television: Gottscho-Schleisner, Inc, photographer, NY, NY, 1950. Photograph. https://www.loc.gov/item/2018723626
Visiting Santa for 1st time: https://www.floridamemory.com/items/show/266487, image is in the public domain.
Joan Wilson confides in Santa: https://www.floridamemory.com/items/show/70682, image is in the public domain.
Boy with polio: https://www.floridamemory.com/items/show/266486, image is in the public domain.
Looking for Santa Claus; https://www.floridamemory.com/items/show/270311, image is in the public domain.
FedEx: photo from San Diego Air & Space Museum, According to the museum, no known restrictions on the publication of photos.
Mickey Mantle: wikimedia commons,1951 Mickey Mantle Original News Photograph, Used for 1951 Bowman Rookie Card, public domain.
Joe Montana: wikimedia commons, 1986 Jeno's Pizza – #28 Roger Craig" card, This work is in the public domain.
Lionel Messi: wikimedia commons, Christopher Johnson, photographer, This work is in the public domain.

For the pictures, special thanks for your help in documenting my life. Love, Santa

shutterstock   LIBRARY OF CONGRESS   WIKIMEDIA COMMONS   PUBLIC DOMAIN   FLORIDA MEMORY State Library and Archives of Florida